To *Andra*

From *Pat + Chrissie*

John B

John Bender

DICK
TRACY
ENCOUNTERS FACEY

by

Paul S. Newman

Authorized Edition

WHITMAN PUBLISHING COMPANY

Racine, Wisconsin

CONTENTS

Facey Smiles Triumphantly

CHAPTER 1

MASTER OF MAKEUP

Facey Fredericks leaned on the glass counter top in the jewelry store and smiled triumphantly. The clerk was wearing a similar gray suit, and that was all that Facey needed to carry out his cunning plot.

A quick glance around the store

with its locked, glass-fronted cabinets, behind which diamonds sparkled, sapphires flashed, and emeralds glowed, convinced Facey that the manager was in the back room displaying some precious jewelry to the woman he had seen entering a few moments before. Facey caught a glimpse of himself in the tilted mirror on the counter. No, the oval face framed by close-cropped brown hair was hardly noticeable in a crowd; he looked like the average man of thirty-five. But this was precisely what made

An Average Man of Thirty-Five

his face worth millions!

"Let's see this ring," Facey requested, tapping commandingly on the glass counter top.

The clerk turned away from the window, in which he had been arranging a glittering necklace.

"Be glad to show it to you, sir," he offered, taking a small key from his pocket. He carefully opened the back of the table cabinet and removed the large, yellow, pear-shaped diamond. It shone magnificently on its platinum setting.

Facey fondled it, held it up to

"Let's See This Ring!"

the light, and studied it.

"What's the price of this?" he asked casually, putting it down on the black velvet display cloth.

"Ah," smiled the clerk. "This is a perfect stone. Flawless. It weighs three and a half carats—"

"The price!" insisted Facey.

"Without tax, it will come to five thousand seven hundred and fifty dollars." The clerk stared intently at Facey to see his reaction.

"Let me write that down," Facey muttered, taking a silver pen from his inside jacket pocket.

Facey Studies the Ring

"My card," the clerk said, placing a small, white business card on the counter top in front of Facey. "Why not use it to make your notes?"

Facey nodded and took another hurried glance about the store. No one was at the door and no one could see him from the back room. Facey raised the pen just above the counter level as the hopeful clerk leaned over. Then he pushed the pen's pocket clip.

POOOOF!

A bluish cloud of smoke shot

Facey Strikes!

upward into the startled clerk's face. Before he could do more than gasp, the clerk's eyes rolled upward and his body slumped down. Facey's hands immediately shot across the counter, catching and supporting the man.

At that moment the front door swung open and two men in dark suits, their faces hidden in the shadows of their downturned hat brims, entered—obviously on cue. They quickly grabbed the unconscious clerk and hurriedly dragged him out of the store.

The Clerk Is Dragged Out of the Store

Facey was already behind the counter, turning the mirror stand around so he could study his face in it. Then he pulled from his jacket pocket makeup tubes, powders, hair coloring, liner pencils, and a tube of adhering, skin-colored plastic.

Deftly, Facey worked. First he broadened his cheekbones to the width of those of the missing clerk. Then his fingertips rubbed coloring through his hair, turning it from brown to black with a hint of gray at the temples. A lining pencil

Facey Applies His Makeup

added forehead wrinkles and shad-
owed his cheeks slightly. Soon his
face was miraculously trans-
formed. Within the startling span
of less than one minute, the missing clerk seemed to once again be
standing at his accustomed place
behind the counter.

"I'll have the clasp readjusted
and call you as soon as it's ready,"
Facey heard the owner say as he
escorted a middle-aged woman past
the counter. Facey nodded to the
customer as the owner solicitously
held open the door for her.

Facey Poses as the Clerk

"She bought it!" exclaimed the owner when the door swung shut. His eyes were sparkling. "It isn't every day that you sell a fifty-thousand-dollar necklace," he marveled.

Facey, mimicking perfectly the departed clerk's voice and inflection, replied, "Wonderful!"

"Now," the owner briskly observed, "we'd better put the trays back in the vault."

It was going along perfectly, Facey thought to himself. He glanced at the front door. One of

"She Bought It!"

his black-suited cronies was light-
ing a cigarette, a signal which
meant the coast was clear. Facey
hurried down the two carpeted
steps and turned into the back
room, where the owner was busily
replacing diamond necklaces in
their velvet-lined cases. Facey
helped him carry the array of val-
uables toward the locked wall safe
whose heavy steel door ran from
ceiling to floor.

The owner reached for the in-
volved combination lock, but before
he turned the numbered dial he

The Jewels Are Carried to the Safe

looked back at his supposed clerk. Anticipating the distrustful glance, Facey had already turned away, pretending to study something on a side table. A moment later, there was a click and the giant door swung open effortlessly.

"Put the things inside," ordered the owner as he stepped into the vault, a chamber ten feet high and twenty feet deep.

At that moment Facey's right hand delivered a vicious karate chop on the back of the owner's neck. With a groan, he sank to the

A Vicious Karate Chop

floor of the jewelry vault.

Facey opened his jacket and un-zipped the top of the lining on both sides. Then into the cleverly pre-pared deep pockets he dropped priceless diamond, ruby, and em-erald baubles.

After a few moments he hurried to the front door of the store and motioned to his two helpers. They carried in the unconscious clerk —Facey's seeming double—and placed him behind the counter in the front room. He groaned. He was regaining consciousness.

Facey Fills His Secret Pockets

"Tracy Here!"

CHAPTER 2

INTERROGATION

At police headquarters a phone rang. Dick Tracy reached for it.

"Tracy here," he said into the receiver.

"A jewel job, Tracy," sighed Chief Patton on the other end. "Jeffer's Jewelry, on Fifth and—"

"I know the place, Chief. Small

store, but very fine, high-priced jewels. Much missing?"

"Over a million. But the thief is still there—and not a jewel on him!"

Dick Tracy hung up. His square jaw set firmly, he hurried out of the station. He was thinking hard. The chief wouldn't have bothered him if it were an ordinary snatch-and-run job. The thief still at the scene of his crime—that did add up to something a bit unusual, especially when he did not have the stolen jewels.

Tracy Rushes Out of the Station

"Jeffer's on Fifth Street," Tracy ordered, sinking down in the front seat of a squad car.

They raced downtown, siren roaring, winding their way through the traffic that cut aside for them. When they pulled up in front of the jewelry store, Tracy saw a sign hanging on the door:

CLOSED

He quickly strode toward the door and knocked firmly.

A uniformed officer opened it and recognized the revered detective at once.

Tracy Arrives at the Jewelry Store

"Detective Tracy," the policeman started to say by way of introduction. The owner hastened at once to Tracy, his hands trembling.

"He did it! That trusted clerk whom I gave a raise to only last week. He did it!" shouted the owner, pointing an accusing finger at the clerk seated dejectedly in front of the counter, a pair of handcuffs encircling his wrists.

"I'm innocent, Mr. Tracy," the clerk stammered. "I know you'll prove that to him."

"Innocent!" roared the owner,

"He Did It!"

rushing toward the clerk. Tracy
stepped quickly but firmly between
them.

"Suppose," Tracy said evenly,
"you tell me why you think he
robbed your store."

"Who else was with me when
I entered the vault?" demanded
the owner. "Only Bob Crockton!
We picked up the necklaces I had
displayed to Mrs. Gould and were
taking them into the vault after I
opened the combination lock. He
was two steps behind me and then
—he struck!"

"Who Else Was With Me?"

"I never—" Crockton started to reply.

"It'll keep," Tracy said to the clerk. He turned again to the owner. "Go on. What happened next?"

"Next," continued the owner, "I came to on the vault floor. My neck was throbbing, my head was spinning, and my vault was looted. Over one million dollars in jewelry was taken, and he did it!"

"I'm innocent," Crockton said with a weary sigh.

"Let me advise you," Tracy said, leaning down to make certain the

"I'm Innocent!"

stunned clerk understood him. "The law does not require you to say a thing. You have the right to ask for a lawyer."

"Maybe that's what I need," agreed Crockton. "You can take me with you, but get me a lawyer. Maybe he'll believe me."

Tracy nodded. The policeman tugged on Crockton's arm and he rose obediently.

"You'll never get him to confess," muttered the owner. "He's too clever!"

As the squad car sped back to

The Clerk Is Led Away

the station, Tracy eyed the passenger slumped next to him.

"I was gassed," Crockton explained. "Someone came in to look at the yellow, pear-shaped diamond engagement ring. He pulled out a pen and gassed me."

"Why not save your alibi for your lawyer," Tracy suggested, not unkindly.

They completed the ride in silence. At the station, charges were made, Crockton was fingerprinted, and a mug shot was taken. Then they waited for Crockton's lawyer.

"Save Your Alibi for Your Lawyer!"

"What do you think, Tracy?" asked Sam Catchem, his assistant and loyal admirer, as he finished studying Crockton's file.

"He wouldn't have been hired in the first place if his references hadn't proved that he was honest," Tracy replied. "Still, the owner's story makes more sense than Crockton's."

"My client is innocent," a silver-haired man called out at that moment. One hand was dramatically placed upon his heart. He was obviously Crockton's attorney.

"What Do You Think, Tracy?"

"Mr. Hammer, we're glad he has convinced you," Tracy replied with a smile of amusement at the attorney's dramatics.

"We are prepared to prove it! Let my client be examined with a lie detector," the attorney proposed.

There was a short conference between Tracy and Chief Patton.

"Okay," replied Tracy. "Let's check him out on the lie detector."

An hour later, in the quiet of Tracy's office, a technician attached the polygraph to Crockton's arm.

"My Client Is Innocent!"

He asked him a few preliminary questions and studied the stylus that recorded his pulse rate on a revolving roll of paper.

"Seems to be working, Tracy," the technician observed. "You can take over."

Sam Catchem, Chief Patton, the lawyer, the technician, and Tracy all stared intently at Crockton as the machine continued to register his reactions.

"Your name?" Tracy asked.

"Robert Crockton."

"Where employed?"

Lie Detector Test

"Jeffer's."

"How long?"

"Just over two years."

"Were you there this morning?"

"Yes."

"Did you show anyone a diamond engagement ring?"

"I did. Man of thirty-five. Hard to describe—average looks."

"Did he use his pen to gas you?"

"He did."

All eyes turned toward the technician. He nodded. According to the machine, Crockton was still speaking the truth.

Tracy Questions Crockton

"Did you enter the vault?" Tracy asked.

"I did not."

"Did you strike your employer?"

"No, I didn't."

"Did you rob the vault or help anyone else rob it?"

"No!"

The technician glanced up from the tape. "He hasn't lied yet," he announced.

"He Hasn't Lied Yet!"

"You've Booked an Innocent Man!"

CHAPTER 3

FACEY STRIKES AGAIN

As Crockton walked out of the station on bail, his attorney paused at the doorway.

"Don't you realize, Tracy," he asked, "that you've booked an innocent man?"

"Mr. Hammer, I know what the lie detector showed—but we both know it isn't legal proof of your client's innocence."

"If you don't come up with some-one else very soon," scoffed the lawyer, "your department will look foolish in court!"

Tracy and Sam saw the pair speed off in a cab.

"Tracy, he could be right."

"Sam," mused Tracy, "let's check that vault for fingerprints. But I'll tell you in advance—I doubt if we'll find any prints be-sides those of the owner and Crock-ton."

"Sam, Let's Check That Vault!"

The print team had already powdered and photographed the interior of the looted vault. When Tracy and Sam arrived, a display of prints was laid out on top of the counter. The police experts were carefully checking them out one by one.

"Negative," the head of the print squad finally concluded. Sam nodded to Tracy. His guess had been correct.

Together, Tracy and Sam recreated the robbery in the manner described by the store owner. Tracy

Print Examination

played the part of the owner, and Sam the part of the clerk.

"He would have heard the door open if someone else had entered," Tracy observed. "And if Crockton was standing just behind him, who else—"

"But Crockton denies doing anything from the time he was gassed till he came to in the chair," Sam noted dryly. "It could be that the owner staged it all while his clerk was out cold and framed him."

Tracy left the store without replying. His mind was suggesting

Not a Single Clue

and rejecting half a dozen possible solutions to the baffling crime. And until he could prove one, he wouldn't offer any solution.

Meanwhile, Facey Fredericks, once again his average self, was being ushered into the large, corner office of J. Dillingworth, president of the Metropolitan Bank. As the guard closed the door behind him, Facey shuffled in seeming awe toward the massive desk behind which sat the bald, distinguished bank official. He was examining

Facey Prepares to Strike Again

a sheaf of legal papers.

"They said you must okay my line of credit, as I'm a new account and wish to take out a substantial—but well-secured—business loan," Facey explained.

Dillingworth smiled and gestured to a chair by the side of the desk. With experienced ease, he examined the form Facey had filled out.

"If you'll just sign it, I'll put it in the pipeline. I should get it back to you by noon tomorrow," he said, starting to offer Facey a handsome

"If You'll Just Sign This!"

pen from his onyx desk set.

"I have my own pen," said Facey, taking out his silver pen. He glanced furtively at the closed office door. The president leaned over to watch him sign.

POOOOF!

There was a slight gasp as the fumes flew into the face of J. Dillingworth. Then he flopped face down on the leather top of his desk.

In an instant Facey was behind the desk, dragging the man from his chair and pushing him unceremoniously into the closet. Then he

Facey's Pen Is Again Effective

hurried over to an antique wall
mirror and, taking his makeup kit
from his pocket, skillfully began
to change his face into that of the
bank president.

When his disguise was complete,
the confident crook went to the
window and raised and lowered the
Venetian blinds twice.

Across the street, a dark-suited
man, his face hidden by his turned-
down hat brim, noted the move-
ment of the Venetian blinds and
hurried down an alley.

Two minutes later there was a

Skillful Disguise

gentle knock on the office door of
J. Dillingworth. An authoritative
voice told the caller to enter.

"Armored car, sir," said a stout,
old guard as he ambled in. "You're
the only one who can authorize this
withdrawal. For one million two
hundred thousand dollars."

"Yes," replied Facey, nodding
and taking the set of triplicate
papers. Looking at J. Dillingworth's signature on a letter that
lay to one side of the massive desk,
the disguised crook quickly and
perfectly forged the president's

"Armored Car, Sir!"

name. The guard took the papers.

"Thanks, Mr. Dillingworth," said the guard, closing the door behind him.

Outside the bank the guard watched as two uniformed men from the armored car stood facing in either direction up the street while the great sum of money in a dozen bags was loaded into the steel encased truck. Then the truck sped off.

From the window of the president's office Facey watched the armored car turn the corner. He

The Money Is Loaded

was busily restoring his face to
that of the innocent caller.

When the disguise was removed,
Facey pulled the still unconscious
J. Dillingworth from the closet and
deposited him gently in his deep
desk chair. Taking a final glance
around to be certain he had left no
clues, and carefully wiping the
door knob as he opened the door,
Facey exited. He quickly mingled
with the busy crowd of noonday
depositors.

Upstairs in his office J. Dillingworth shook his head and blinked.

Facey Pulls Dillingworth From the Closet

He sat up and gazed around the empty room. His fingers rubbed his temples as he tried to recall what had happened.

"Must have blacked out," he muttered to himself. "The doctor warned me about overwork."

At that moment, the armored car withdrawal receipt which was lying on his desk caught his eye. He noted the amount and the forged signature. "Robbery!" he gasped.

"Must Have Blacked Out!"

"Sounds Like the Same Pattern!"

CHAPTER 4

NO CLUES

"Sounds like the same pattern," Sam Catchem offered as he and Dick Tracy sped in Tracy's car toward the bank.

"We'll know more when we get there, Sam," Tracy cautioned. But he realized that the bank job and the jewelry store heist had several features in common.

Tracy pulled alongside the NO PARKING sign outside the bank and nodded to the policeman at the corner as he climbed from his car.

The old bank guard, puffing from excitement, led them up the short flight of stairs to J. Dillingworth's office.

"Over a million dollars—gone!" sighed the president as Tracy and Sam sat down. "But I know I didn't sign that withdrawal slip."

Sam carefully compared the signature on the withdrawal slip with

In Front of the Bank

the president's signature on a
letter.

"Offhand, they look awfully
much alike, Mr. Dillingworth,"
Sam concluded.

"Do you imagine I'd rob my own
bank?" stormed the distraught
official.

"Someone did," Tracy stated in
a low voice. "If we may borrow
some of your papers, perhaps we
can find the crook."

As Sam collected the needed
documents, Tracy checked the
closet.

"I Didn't Sign Anything!"

"What did the man you say was here look like?"

"Well . . . it's rather hard to say. Thirty-five to forty . . . brown hair . . . average build and face. In fact, he had the kind of face you'd never notice in a crowd."

"What was he wearing?" Tracy asked.

"I can remember that clearly. The reason's simple—he was wearing a dark, pinstriped suit almost identical to mine!"

"Thank you, Mr. Dillingworth. Only one more thing. If you're

"What Did the Man Look Like?"

planning to leave town, please contact me first."

"Leave town!" exclaimed the official. "Don't you think I realize that bank robbery is a federal offense? I know that government inspectors will be down here within the hour. But I *didn't* sign that receipt."

Tracy smiled reassuringly as he closed the door behind him.

"That signature could send him up for a long stretch," Sam murmured as they walked down the corridor.

Tracy and Sam Leave

"Let's check it out first," Tracy replied thoughtfully.

"Focus it more clearly," Tracy requested. He was sitting next to Sam in the darkened projection room of the police station. A stereo projector with dual mounts was focusing two signatures in an overlapping pattern on the screen. One signature was Dillingworth's at the end of a letter and the other was the signature on the withdrawal receipt. Slowly, carefully, the skilled police technician was

Comparing the Signatures

matching the two signatures.

"No," declared Tracy, "they look identical, but Dillingworth doesn't make his lower 'g' loop like the one on the receipt."

Sam studied the projection for another moment and then nodded his head in agreement. "It was a good forging job, though, fast and professional—"

"But it couldn't fool the stereo projector," Tracy finished, flicking on the room lights.

"Chief wants you, Tracy," a policeman said, poking his head

"It Was a Good Forging Job!"

into the projection room. Tracy
and Sam hurried to Chief Patton's office.

"Better get down to Grove
Street," Patton said tersely.
"They just found the armored car
—empty."

Fifteen minutes later Tracy and
Sam pulled up behind the armored
truck which was parked at the curb
of a deserted slum street. A policeman stood on guard, and inside the
steel-protected truck a fingerprint
team was already at work. Tracy
stuck his head into the armored

The Empty Armored Car

car, and one of the technical team looked up.

"Real pros, Tracy," he muttered. "They didn't leave a thing—not even a smudge of a print."

"You checked the wheel, the gas-tank cap—" the detective began.

"Tracy, I even checked under the hood," the man sighed.

As Tracy returned to his car he flicked on his two-way wrist TV.

"Chief," he said when Patton's burly face came into focus on the miniature screen, "get me a ten twenty-eight on the armored car's

Tracy Reports to the Chief

license. The number is SV eight-seven-nine."

"I'll have it for you before you're back," the chief assured him.

Sam sat staring at the truck. "A smart, well-timed job. It doesn't make sense that in one day the same creep would pull the jewelry job and then hit the bank."

"It would," said Tracy as he started the car, "if he wasn't working on his own, but was hired by others for his talents at disguise."

"You mean, we may be looking for one character who worked for

"A Smart, Well-Timed Job!"

two gangs today?"

"It is possible, Sam."

The empty money bags, all stamped with the words METRO-POLITAN BANK, lay in the back room of a pet store. The room was lined with aquariums in which colorful fish darted about, hardly noticing the four men who sat at the round table counting money. Facey watched the men with fascination, perspiration glinting on his forehead.

"Here's your cut, Facey," said

Dividing the Loot

a cigar puffing crook in dapper clothes. Facey nodded in silent approval as he stuffed the large sum of money into his pocket.

"You pulled a neat job with that disguise. And being a forger didn't hurt, either," said the leader. "The boys left the car clean. We're safe. And, Facey, I'm going to recommend you to some of the big guys. You won't be unemployed long. Not with your cute little talent for disguise!"

Facey smiled and strode to the door.

Facey Gets His Cut

Patton Studies Tracy

CHAPTER 5

A WOUNDED WITNESS

At headquarters, Patton looked squarely at Tracy. "Insisting Dillingworth is innocent sure puts you out on a limb," he said darkly.

Chief Patton studied Tracy for a moment. From the hard set of his jaw, he knew that Tracy's mind was made up.

"Do you realize," continued the chief, "that the federal bank authorities are clamoring for an arrest?"

"Even if the man's innocent?"

"Look, Tracy, it has all the earmarks of an inside job. Dillingworth's story is kind of hard to take."

"It wasn't for me, Chief, not after checking out those signatures."

Patton patted Tracy on the back. Long years of professional association had proven to him that

The Chief Understands

Dick Tracy did not give in easily.

"Sleep on it," suggested Patton.

Facey Fredericks suddenly woke up in a cold sweat. He quickly rose from the Japanese bed which lay flat on the floor mat, and turned on the lights in his studio apartment. The room was tastefully hung with Japanese silk-screen paintings and furnished with lacquered, Oriental furniture. Facey hurried toward the closet door. There, his hands searched hopefully through the pockets of both suits he had worn

Facey Searches Through His Suits

that eventful and profitable day. He turned the pockets inside out. Then he slumped down into a low chair, his head in his hands.

"I left it there," he groaned. "I was so excited, I must have left it right there on that bank president's desk."

He took a few paces around the room. He was a man plunged from sudden success into utter despair.

"If the cops find it—no! I've got to go back and retrieve my silver gas-pen from Dillingworth's office tomorrow. Don't know how . . . but

"I've Got to Retrieve My Gas-Pen!"

if I don't get into that office I'll end up behind bars!"

At twelve o'clock the next day Facey Fredericks sat huddled in his car across the street from the Metropolitan Bank.

"He must surely go out for lunch," he mused, trying to console himself. Suddenly his eyes lit up. Striding out of the front door the guard held open for him was J. Dillingworth!

Facey took another look into the car mirror and touched up his

Facey Waits Anxiously

cheek line with a dark makeup
pencil. Then out of Facey's car
emerged a second "J. Dillingworth."

"No," thought Facey, ducking
back into the car. "I'd better not
go in so soon."

Agonizingly he watched ten
minutes pass on the bank's big
clock. Then he boldly made for the
front door. As he entered the
massive bank, he felt that all eyes
were on him. He nodded confidently
to a smiling teller, waved to an
executive at a desk in the mortgage

Facey Enters the Bank in Disguise

department, and at last started up the stairs to "his" private office. As he opened the door he noted the old guard looking up at him from the vault's stairwell a flight below. He quickly entered the office and closed the door behind him. The room was deserted; everything seemed in quiet order. Facey went straight to the desk. The gas-pen was not lying on top of it. Cautiously he opened the big middle drawer. Several bottles of pills and some pencils rattled as the drawer was pulled back. The gas-pen was

He Searches for His Gas-Pen

not there. He tried another drawer; it was locked. He did not want to force it—yet. Then he saw it! He smiled triumphantly. There was his silver pen, nestled in a round pen and pencil holder to one side of the desk, crowded among two dozen other pens and pencils! Facey took it quickly, realizing that Dillingworth's secretary or someone had innocently assumed it to be the president's and had replaced it among his other writing tools.

"What a piece of luck!" he murmured half aloud. Then his eyes

"What a Piece of Luck!"

turned toward the door. The knock he had heard was repeated. His first thought was to hide, but then he realized he could easily bluff it out.

"Come in," he said, imitating the official's voice.

The door swung open and the old bank guard entered.

"Thought I saw you come back, Mr. Dillingworth," he exclaimed as he closed the door behind him. "Weren't out long, were you, sir?"

"Forgot something," Facey said with a friendly smile.

"Weren't Out Long, Were You, Sir?"

"Mr. Dillingworth, are my old eyes playing tricks or didn't you leave in a brown suit, while now you're wearing—"

"Your eyes must be playing tricks!" Facey stated boldly. "I have been wearing this pinstriped suit all day."

He started for the door.

"Just a minute, sir," the guard said, barring the way to the door. "Mind telling me my nickname?"

"Look, I haven't time for childish games," raged Facey.

Before he could take another

"Just a Minute, Sir!"

step forward, the guard drew his pistol. Facey pressed the clip of the gas-pen, which he still held in his hand. The guard saw the fumes starting for his face and stepped aside. But he was momentarily diverted, long enough for Facey to grab the hand that held the gun. The two men wrestled desperately for a few moments. Then Facey turned the guard's wrist.

BANG!

The guard groaned and slumped to the floor, grasping his side in great pain.

Facey and the Guard Struggle

Facey darted for the door and locked it. In an instant he was out the window and starting down the fire escape.

Twenty minutes later Dick Tracy and Sam Catchem saw the ambulance crew carry the guard by on a stretcher. "Who shot you?" Tracy asked the guard gently.

"Dillingworth . . . the man was—" But he sank into unconsciousness before he could say another word.

"Who Shot You?"

"Here Comes the Man He Named!"

CHAPTER 6

HAS TRACY FLIPPED?

The wounded guard's words echoed in their ears as Tracy and Sam watched the ambulance speed off.

"Here comes the man he named," exclaimed Sam in surprise as they saw J. Dillingworth stride to the bank. Tracy nodded and hurried toward the bank official.

"Mr. Dillingworth, I'm sorry to inform you that you'd better come along with us now to headquarters."

The bank official looked at them with stunned disbelief. Tracy quickly explained what had happened as he ushered Dillingworth into a car.

"But I was out shopping," the man stammered. "It's my wife's birthday."

"Funny," muttered Sam. "He could be the first man ever found

"But I Was Out Shopping!"

guilty for remembering his wife's birthday!"

When the car arrived at the station, Chief Patton took over the questioning. Tracy and Sam returned to the bank with some special equipment.

"Diet Smith rigged this lamp for me," Tracy explained as he set up two bluish-colored, pear-shaped bulbs on low portable floor stands in Dillingworth's office. "I asked him for a way to spot shoe prints on carpeting, and he worked out an ultraviolet shadow scope light."

The Ultraviolet Shadow Scope Light

Tracy pressed the switch and the thick carpeting was bathed in an eerie purple light. Across the carpet they now saw countless shoe impressions. Tracy handed Sam a small stereo camera. Slowly, laboriously, Sam began photographing every set of shoe prints on the carpet.

While Sam was at work, Tracy had Mr. Dillingworth's secretary assemble everyone who had been in the office during the past twenty-four hours. Tracy then took tracings of everyone's shoes.

Sam Photographs the Footprints

By the end of the day, Tracy and Sam had completed their tasks. They now matched the shoe tracings with the stereo prints taken from the carpet. Sixty-four of the sixty-five shoe prints checked out. Now they had the prints of the intruder!

"Call in Junior," Tracy commanded.

Into the lab came Junior, his youthful face serious.

"Junior, you've proven yourself at sketching the faces of wanted men from the victims' descriptions.

Tracy Calls In Junior

This time I want you to sketch a shoe from its track."

"Gosh," exclaimed Junior, "I'll try. But this won't be easy."

The next day Junior spent his time consulting a local shoe manufacturer and sketching. Finally he confidently handed Tracy a sketch.

"The one unmatched shoe print," Junior declared, "was made by a special shoe. I checked it out with a shoe manufacturer, who says the pair of shoes in question was specially made. They have an elevator lift on the heels to make the wearer

Junior Shows the Sketch to Tracy

a few inches taller, and a support on the inner arch. Building up a shoe from the print gives us one that should look like this."

Dick Tracy studied the drawing of the special shoe.

"Shouldn't be too hard to track down," he commented. "Put it in the active file. Tomorrow we'll run off flyers and send the men around to check the shoe stores. Oh, and, Junior, that's a great piece of workmanship there."

Junior beamed as he put the valuable sketch in the files.

Tracy Examines the Drawing

Chief Patton was desperately trying to fend off the press.

"You booked a bank president," shrilled one reporter. "The case must be hot! Any breaks?"

"None," the Chief said shortly.

"Come on, Patton," coaxed another reporter. "You let Dillingworth out on bail. You must have some lead."

The barrage of questions continued until Patton raised his hand for silence. "All right! Tracy has a lead. Junior made a sketch of a special shoe that was taken

Reporters Question the Chief

from a stereo print of all the shoe prints in the bank president's office. That print and Junior's reconstruction of the shoe may be the big break that'll tell us who the unknown caller was at Dillingworth's office. We'll check it out in the morning. The shoe stores are closed now. And it's quitting time for me, too."

With that, the chief strode through the pack of reporters.

That night, sitting cross-legged on his floor and eating from his

The Chief Strides Out

low Japanese table, Facey stared at the late edition of the paper.

"My shoes! Those blasted coppers have a sketch of my special shoes! If they circulate it, they'll find my shoemaker and nab me! Wait . . . I've got a chance, after all." He chuckled softly.

The next morning Sam turned as Tracy entered the station.

"Early, aren't you?" he asked.

"Get me the shoe file, all exhibits," Tracy ordered.

Sam shrugged and went off. A

"Get Me the Shoe File!"

moment later he returned with the folder containing the stereo slides, tracings of the shoe prints, and Junior's sketch. Silently, Tracy took them from him and started for the door.

"Hey!" exclaimed Sam. "You know that even you can't remove an exhibit from headquarters."

"I'll bring it right back," replied Tracy.

Sam grabbed him by the arm. "Hold on. I won't let you get yourself into a mess of trouble—"

With his free hand, Tracy swung

Sam Tries to Stop Tracy

swiftly and accurately. The karate chop caught Sam on the side of the neck, and he fell with a groan.

"Tracy, have you flipped?" exclaimed a policeman, who was passing by on his way off duty. Again, Tracy's hand whistled through the air, and the policeman sank to the floor.

A minute later as Sam and the officer were pulling themselves up off the floor, they looked at the door in amazement. Dick Tracy was entering! They suddenly realized what had happened.

Facey, as Tracy, Strikes Again!

'He's a Clever Makeup Artist!'

CHAPTER 7

A GRIM HOAX

Tracy watched Sam hold the ice pack against his aching neck.

"A very clever makeup artist is our man," Tracy concluded.

"One who knows karate, too," Sam added. "Probably learned it in Japan. He was good."

"With the shoe slides, tracings,

and sketches gone," Tracy continued, "we've lost our best lead. But Junior worried him once. Maybe we can use Junior to finger him again."

Tracy pushed back his jacket sleeve and worked the dials on his two-way wrist TV set. Junior's sleepy face came into focus. "Yes?"

"Junior, I'm going to bring in Dillingworth and the jewelry store clerk. Let's see if you can get enough information from them to sketch the man behind the masks!"

Sam smiled as the miniature TV

Tracy Contacts Junior

screen went blank. "If I remember correctly, both victims of that gas-pen claimed he was awfully non-descript looking. How does Junior draw that?"

"Your two-hundred-thousand-dollar life insurance policy has been approved, Mr. Wently," commented the insurance broker with a smile. He sat in his office facing Mr. Wently, a trim man in his mid-thirties with wavy red hair. His attractive and younger-looking blonde wife sat at his side.

"Your Policy Has Been Approved!"

"It gives me the creeps, talking about Wendell's dying like this," the woman said in a low, pleasant voice.

"Perfectly understandable, Mrs. Wently," the broker assured her. "But if anything did happen to your husband, wouldn't he want you well provided for?"

"Of course, I would, dear," Mr. Wently said, squeezing her hand.

"The premium is a little high because you fly your own plane, Mr. Wently," the broker explained.

"Here's your check," said the

"It's for Your Protection, Dear!"

red-haired client. "I'm ready to pay a little extra to keep on enjoying my one hobby."

"Oh, Wendell, I do wish you would give it up."

"We've been through this before, dear," he replied, rising.

A few moments later Mr. and Mrs. Wently drove off. Mrs. Wently was at the wheel. Mr. Wently was busy removing his red wig, applying cold cream to remove facial lines and freckles, and pulling off the putty that had built up his nose. Facey then turned to the woman.

Facey Removes His Makeup

"Went like a charm," he commented happily.

"Yeah, but it gets grim from here on, honey."

"Forty grand will help you forget that," he soothed.

Since his successful impersonation of Dick Tracy at police headquarters, Facey's confidence knew no bounds. The car stopped at his apartment house.

"Meet you tomorrow night at five sharp—don't be late," he said as he climbed out.

"I know, I know. We have to be

"Went Like a Charm!"

outside Wendell's weekend place at seven sharp if we're going to kidnap him and pull off this little caper." She jammed down on the gas pedal and sped off.

Facey entered his apartment and tossed the insurance policy on the table. In a few days he'd be a hundred and sixty thousand dollars richer, thanks to his ordinary—but highly changeable—face!

"Select the basic head shape," Junior suggested as J. Dillingworth and the jewelry store clerk

Facey Returns to His Apartment

studied half a dozen facial shapes
on Junior's drawing board. They
included almost every shape of the
human head. Yet the two men
could not immediately agree on
which was the shape of their gas-
pen assailant's head.

"Round jaw like this drawing,"
declared Dillingworth positively.

"I think," contradicted the clerk
softly, "it was a little longer."

For two hours Junior worked at
the drawing board, altering, chang-
ing, shading, correcting, and ad-
justing his sketch of the crook to

They Study Junior's Sketches

meet the seemingly endless sugges-
tions of the two victims. When he
completed the drawing, neither
man was completely satisfied, but
both agreed there was a certain
likeness to their attacker in the
sketch that lay on Junior's drawing board.

Tracy studied the face. "Not
much to go on. I've seen a thousand
faces like this in any crowd—which
is this disguise artist's chief asset."

Not wanting to overlook any
possible lead, Tracy ordered photos
made of the suspect's sketch and

"I've Seen a Thousand Faces Like This!"

had them distributed to his detective squad.

"I see what you mean," Sam commented when he saw the sketch. "Not much to go on. We've got a lot more leg work ahead of us before we nab this cutie."

One karate chop and Wendell Wently never knew what hit him as he passed the tall bushes at his weekend country home. He fell like a weighted sack. Facey and the blonde dumped him into a car and sped off.

Thud!

The disguised Facey signed out for his flight at the small local airport and then went to Wently's two-seater. He taxied it down the field to where a darkened car waited. Quickly the unconscious man was shoved aboard.

Taking the controls, a parachute on his back, Facey gunned the engine and zoomed skyward.

At five thousand feet he stalled the motor and the plane began to vibrate wildly. Slipping Wently into the pilot's seat, Facey flung open the door of the plane. He took

Facey Flies Wentiy's Plane

a last, satisfied glance at the man whose face he wore and dove out into the night.

A hard tug and his chute opened. As he drifted down Facey saw the plane nose over, shake, and plunge into a hillside with an explosive roar.

He landed in the field where the blonde had parked the car.

"How's it feel to be a rich widow?" he asked with a laugh as he tore off his Wently disguise.

Facey Parachutes to Safety

Tracy and Sam Examine the Wreckage

CHAPTER 8

FACEY IS IDENTIFIED

A few days later, after the insurance claim had been checked and paid, Dick Tracy stood by the plane wreckage with Sam. "Two men went up in it—only one came down," he said.

Sam looked at the wreckage, which was roped off and protected

by the federal aviation authorities.
He nodded his head in agreement.
Clothing fibers had been found on
both seats of the smashed plane.
Yet only one body had been taken
from the wreckage—Wendell
Wently.

"What happened to the other
guy?" asked Sam wonderingly.

They returned silently to their
car. Tracy had an idea. He needed
Junior's skillful sketching hand
again.

"Junior," Tracy said back at the
station, "assume that the missing

"What Happened to the Other Guy?"

man was made up as Wently. I want you to draw the following faces—Dillingworth's, the jewelry store clerk's, Wently's, and mine. If I am right, behind all those imitated faces is a face that will stand up as the disguise artist's!"

Hours later, by projecting all the faces on a screen at once and shaping and shading features, Junior came up with a final composite face to show to Dillingworth and the jewelry store clerk.

"That's him!" shouted the bank official excitedly.

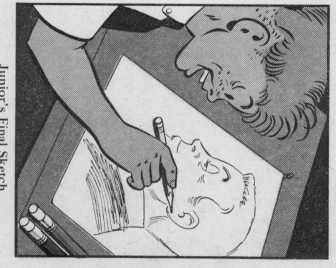

Junior's Final Sketch

The jeweler remained silent as all eyes turned to him. "If the nose were a bit wider ... no! That is the man who gassed me," he finally declared.

Tracy gave Junior a hearty congratulatory pat on the back and hurried off with the sketch.

Warren Baymore looked through his horn-rimmed glasses as he sat back in the deep chair of his theatrical booking agency. The walls in his office were lined with photos of movie and television stars. They

Tracy Tries to Trace Facey

all seemed to be looking at him, Tracy thought to himself.

"Yes!" exclaimed Baymore suddenly, snapping his fingers in recollection. "Now I know who this reminds me of—Freddy Fredericks. We called him 'Facey' because he was a master of makeup. I tried booking him for two years—no luck. He left my agency about a year and a half ago. Don't think he ever made it as an actor. He was a good voice mimic, but his real specialty was as a makeup artist."

"Do you have any pictures of this

Baymore Recognizes Facey

Fredericks?" Tracy inquired.

Baymore hurried to a big file cabinet and started rummaging through his clients' folders. He pulled out one.

"Here's Facey's file. Funny, not a single photo of him in it!"

"The sketch will do," Tracy said. "Have his address?"

Baymore scribbled out a house number and handed the note to Tracy. The detective shook hands gratefully and strode out onto the street.

Quickly he tuned in his two-way

"Here's Facey's File!"

wrist TV to Chief Patton. The chief's face came into focus on the tiny television screen almost immediately. "Chief, I want a pickup at two twenty-three Larkspur Road. Facey Fredericks. Suspect in bank robbery, jewel theft, and murder!"

Then Tracy climbed into a car. Sam was waiting at the wheel. As they sped along to meet the squad car at Fredericks' building, Tracy quickly brought Sam up to date on the latest lead.

"Then Junior's sketch and your

Tracy Orders a Pickup

hunch have paid off, Tracy!"

"Save the congratulations, Sam, till a jury confirms it."

Tat! TAT-ATTTAAT!!

The clatter of a tommy gun was loud and distinct as their car raced around the corner of Larkspur Road.

"Shooting!" exclaimed Tracy. Sam pulled hard on the wheel and jammed on the brakes, and they skidded to a stop by the curb. Up ahead, three uniformed officers were firing over the hood of their parked squad car. Down from a

Gun Fight

second-floor window came a stream of tommy-gun slugs. Tracy and Sam drew their service revolvers.

"What's happening?" Tracy called out.

"Keep back, Tracy," replied an officer. "Whoever this Facey Fredericks is, he's got some gun-happy pals! They got the sergeant."

PLUNMMMPH!

The tear gas pellet someone had fired from the window landed alongside the squad car just as Tracy and Sam were joining the officers there. In seconds, the fumes

Tear Gas!

were over all of them. Tracy
hugged a handkerchief to his face
and rushed from the stinging gas
cloud. His eyes were teary, his
breath was coming in choking
gasps, and he couldn't see a dozen
feet ahead of him.

By the time the pellet had
stopped fuming, the tommy gun at
the window had vanished. Sam and
Tracy raced for the door. Just
outside lay the wounded police
sergeant.

"Gone!" muttered Tracy as he
looked around the empty studio

Tracy Is Enveloped in the Fumes

apartment with its Japanese furnishings.

Using his two-way wrist TV, Tracy signaled for an ambulance and put out a 10-40 alert for the escaped Fredericks and his arsenal-armed companions.

"Nothing," reported Sam as he finished checking the apartment.

"I'm more concerned about who Facey left with," remarked Tracy. "Assuming we now know our man, the real question is, what gang helped Facey shoot his way out of here? If some of the big crime boys

The Apartment Was Empty

are protecting Facey, they must need him for a big job. What is it?"

In the hideout room behind the pet store, Facey and four dark-suited gangland hoodlums looked at a moustached man's face which filled their TV screen. He was David Davis, official city greeter, who was explaining how he would welcome Princess Faida from Perestan on her arrival tomorrow. As he watched, Facey was busily putting on makeup until he was David Davis' living double!

Facey Prepares for His Next Role

A Dart Strikes Home

CHAPTER 9

A HANDSOME RETURN

At eight o'clock David Davis opened the window of his suburban country home to inhale the fresh morning air.

TWIIICK!

The tiny dart struck him in the chest and he sank to the carpeted floor of his bachelor bedroom.

From the thick shrubbery, a dark-suited man emerged, holstering his dart gun. He beckoned to Facey, who followed him into the house through the open window.

They turned Davis over. He was breathing gently.

"That tranquilizer dart will keep him out for at least five hours," the hoodlum noted.

"Do we match?" asked Facey, smoothing his artificial moustache. The hoodlum glanced from the unconscious Davis to his conscious double, then whistled admiringly.

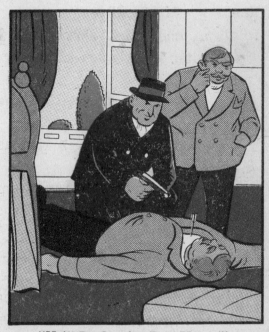

"He'll Be Out for Five Hours!"

An hour later Facey was seated in the back of a shiny chauffeur-driven limousine speeding to the airport.

Once there, Facey stood with the other notables waiting to greet the twenty-year-old princess from the oil-rich land as she emerged from her father's private four-engine jetliner. Flashbulbs popped, celebrities spoke, and Facey handed her a beautiful bouquet. Then he escorted her to his car and they drove toward the city, where leading citizens would greet and lunch with

A Disguised Facey Greets the Princess

her. The princess smiled at her
moustached companion as they
sped along. Suddenly, from either
shoulder of the highway, two armored cars roared onto the road
just behind the princess' car. The
police escort and cavalcade of six
limousines that were following her
slammed to a halt, their way barred
by the burly armored cars. The
chauffeur glanced in the rearview
mirror in stunned surprise as he
saw bullets stream from the armored cars' gun slits, cutting down
the startled police escort.

He Escorts Her in His Limousine

"Keep driving! I'll tell you where to go," Facey said, shoving a pistol's cold nose into the back of the neck of the helpless chauffeur.

Their car sped on. Two motor-cyclists in black outfits, goggles masking their faces, sped in from a side road to guide them.

"Follow them!" Facey ordered the driver.

Behind their limousine, a short, sharp battle raged. From the steel protection of their armored cars, the thugs easily shot down the escorting police motorcyclists. The

"Follow Them!"

two or three wounded officers who tried firing back from the highway where they had fallen came under a quick hail of bullets from the armored cars' gun slits. Above, a police helicopter surveying the startling kidnapping alerted headquarters.

Splatt! SPLATT!

Tommy-gun slugs stitched the chopper's glass hull and snapped its rotors.

"We're going down," gasped the police pilot. With a great splash, the copter plunged into the river.

The Police Helicopter Is Shot Down

A moment later two badly shaken police pilots surfaced and clung to the wreckage. In the distance they could see the princess' limousine swing off the highway and make its safe escape.

Two hours later, after Dick Tracy and Sam Catchem had climbed through the still open window of David Davis' bedroom, the pieces of the puzzle began to fit together.

"Davis was here, not at the airport," murmured Sam as they

"Davis Was Right Here!"

observed the peacefully sleeping city greeter.

"I was watching her arrival on TV," Tracy commented. "The princess was greeted by Davis' double. That must have been Facey's handiwork again."

Sam nodded in agreement.

"And that explains why someone sent an armed escort for that out-of-work actor yesterday. This was the job some gang needed Facey for. And if we don't find—"

A signal beeped on Tracy's two-way wrist TV. Chief Patton's

"This Is More of Facey's Handiwork!"

angry face filled its screen.

"The ransom message just came in for the princess—five million!"

"Five million!" echoed Tracy.

"They say her father is very, very rich. This is embarrassing our country internationally. Facey's pals made it look like we can't protect foreign visitors from our own criminals. Find her—and fast!" The tiny screen went blank.

"Sam," sighed Tracy, "let's turn this place upside-down for clues. The gang might have come here from their hideout. I want this

"Find Her—and Fast!"

room vacuumed and the dirt analyzed!"

Six hours later Tracy and Sam stood in the police crime lab. A technician was shaking a test tube over a low flame.

"Positive reaction, Tracy," he exclaimed. "The sand grains found in Davis' room came from an area where there is a high silicon con-centration. Our geologist suggests Crater Canyon."

Quickly, Tracy and Sam went to a wall map, where the technician pinpointed the canyon some sixty-

"Positive Reaction, Tracy!"

five miles from the city in a rugged area. An assistant handed them a file of aerial photos of the canyon. Tracy studied them carefully.

"If we try to get in by the only overland trail, they could hold off an army in that ravine. If we try going in by copter, they could threaten to shoot the princess. But there is one way to get in—a risky way!" Tracy squared his shoulders defiantly.

The police plane flew high over the canyon at nine o'clock that

"There Is Only One Way to Get In!"

night. The pilot signaled. Out the hatch dove two parachuted figures —Dick Tracy and Sam Catchem. They were going to sky dive, not opening their chutes till the last moment, in hopes that they might land in the canyon unseen. Sam glanced at Tracy as they fell. Tracy was made up to match Junior's sketch of Facey. If that sketch wasn't accurate, Tracy was a doomed double!

"Let's Go!"

A Silent Drop

CHAPTER 10

DOUBLE TROUBLE

Just above the canyon rim two parachutes flared open. Tracy and Sam swung beneath their dark, camouflaged canopies. Moments later they hit a grassy slope inside the canyon, rolled, and landed safely.

They unstrapped, tossed the

chutes into the brush, and started for the large cavern tucked into the canyon wall. They could see a light inside the cavern.

"That must be their hideout," whispered Tracy.

Sam nodded and the two men moved on silently. They ducked low near some bushes when they were only a hundred yards from the cavern and studied the figures moving back and forth inside the entrance. There were at least a dozen men in the gang. The odds were strongly against them unless

"That Must Be Their Hideout!"

Tracy's disguise was successful.

Sam drew his revolver to cover Tracy as the detective moved forward. A guard was patrolling the cavern entrance. Tracy walked boldly up to him.

"All okay?" he asked.

"Sure, Facey," replied the guard.

The disguise had worked!

"How's the princess?"

"Still refusing to eat. Maybe you can convince her, Facey," the guard replied, jerking a thumb toward the cavern, where the princess

The Disguise Works

apparently was being held.

Tracy moved on to the rear of the cavern. There the long-haired princess sat on a wooden crate. Her pretty nose was turned up at the platter of food in front of her. A hoodlum, cradling a tommy gun, stood over her.

"Let me talk her into eating," said Tracy, waving the guard aside. The man walked slowly to the cavern entrance.

"I won't eat till I am released," protested the determined princess.

"Eat and listen to me," Tracy

"Eat and Listen to Me!"

said softly, in his own voice.

Quickly he whispered who he was and his daring plan. Suspicious at first, the princess accepted his word when she realized his voice was not that of the man he was made up to look like.

Tracy flicked on his two-way wrist TV. A helicopter pilot's face flickered on the screen.

"Bring in the chopper. We're going to our station," he whispered.

Then Tracy and the princess walked casually to the cavern entrance. But just then the real

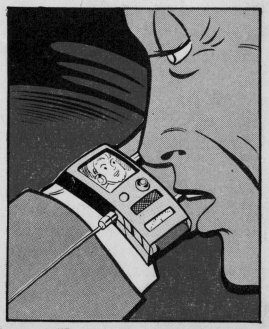

"Bring in the Chopper!"

Facey appeared. The startled hoodlums looked from one Facey to the other.

"Grab him!" shouted Tracy. "He must be a cop made up to impersonate me! Get that dirty copper!"

The hoods turned for the real Facey.

"Stop, you fools," screamed Facey. "He's the phony—not me!"

"Yank off his disguise," commanded Tracy.

The hoodlums rushed for a punching and shouting Facey. They pinned his arms and then

Two Faceys!

tugged on his hair and face, trying to rip off a wig and makeup.

During the wild confusion, Tracy hustled the princess outside to where Sam stood.

"Now," ordered Tracy.

Sam tossed a smoke grenade between them and the fighting hoodlums and Facey.

POOOOF!

The grenade exploded a cloud of thick, masking white smoke.

"Now do you believe me?" Tracy and Sam heard Facey shout. He was half-choking on the smoke.

Sam Tosses a Smoke Grenade

"Don't let that copper escape with our five million dollar princess!"

The hoodlums began firing wildly through the smoke. Sam blazed back, and soon a gasp of pain indicated that his shots had found a target. Above the sound of gunfire, the whirling rotors of a chopper could be heard.

"Here comes the lifeline," Tracy called.

Swinging toward them from the low-flying helicopter was a sling. As Sam continued to fire into the smoke to force back the thugs,

"Here Comes the Lifeline!"

Tracy slipped the yoke under the princess' arms.

"What about you two?" she asked.

"We'll grab on!" Tracy replied. He and Sam clung to the rope with one hand, at the same time firing the revolvers held in their other hands.

The copter began to rise and haul in the sling and the three suspended figures.

"There they are!" shouted Facey as he and his men rushed from the thinning smoke cloud. Guns swept

The Copter Begins to Rise

skyward. But the policeman in the copter had already tossed down a tear gas grenade. The hoodlums fired blindly as the copter sped off.

Minutes later, with the princess safely seated inside the chopper, Tracy looked at Chief Patton's face on his two-way wrist TV.

"Okay, Chief, she's out. Move in!" Tracy advised.

An armored police car soon raced into the canyon with a machine gun blazing. And over the canyon rim climbed riot police. The gang was hopelessly surrounded. They

"Chief, She's Out. Move In!"

quickly surrendered.

Two hours later the hoodlums were lined up at police headquarters. Tracy, Sam, and Patton surveyed the sorry lot.

"But Facey got away," muttered Patton, holding up Junior's sketch.

"Clean them up," suggested Tracy. "Have them all go through a steam bath."

At first Patton looked puzzled. Then he smiled knowingly.

In a few minutes there was shouting from the steam bath.

"Where's Facey?"

"Let me out of here!" one hoodlum was screaming.

It was too late. His false features had been dissolved by the heat, as Tracy had anticipated, and Facey was finally exposed.

Tracy soon shoved Facey in front of the mug shot camera.

Click! The disguise artist was photographed for all time. The crook of a dozen faces was just another face in a police file marked —SOLVED!

"Goodnight, Chief," Tracy said simply and started home.

The Case Was Solved

Other **BIG LITTLE BOOKS** Available

WHITMAN Tween-Age Books

Easy to Read . . . Full of Fun and Adventure

Books About Animals

GOLDEN PRIZE—Stories About Horses

HERE, BOY!—Stories About Dogs

THAT'S OUR CLEO!—Stories About Cats

Old Favorites

TALES FROM THE ARABIAN NIGHTS

TALES FROM HANS CHRISTIAN ANDERSEN

Adventure

ADVENTURES WITH HAL

DONALD DUCK AND THE LOST MESA RANCH

DORY BOY

IT'S A MYSTERY!

MYSTERY AT REDTOP HILL

WHITMAN *Big Book Adventures*

Based on famous TV shows

I SPY

THE GREEN HORNET

THE MAN FROM U.N.C.L.E.

BONANZA

LASSIE

FLIPPER

THE BIG VALLEY

PATTY DUKE

GILLIGAN'S ISLAND

VOYAGE TO THE BOTTOM OF THE SEA